Like a
Hundred
Drums

Like a Hundred Drums

BY ANNETTE GRIESSMAN

ILLUSTRATED BY JULIE MONKS

Houghton Mifflin Company
BOSTON 2006

www.houghtonmifflinbooks.com

The text of this book is set in 15-point ITC Usherwood Medium.
The illustrations are done using oil paint, pastels, and crayon.
Book design by Carol Goldenberg

Library of Congress Cataloging-in-Publication Data

Griessman, Annette.
Like a hundred drums / written by Annette Griessman ; illustrated by Julie Monks.
p. cm.
Summary: Children, their grandmother, and various animals
sense the excitement of an approaching thunderstorm.
ISBN 0-618-55878-0 (hardcover)
[1. Thunderstorms—Fiction. 2. Animals—Fiction. 3. Grandmothers—Fiction.]
I. Monks, Julie, ill. II. Title.
PZ7.G881235Li 2006
[E]—dc22
2004026551
ISBN-13: 978-0618-55878-0

Printed in Singapore
TWP 10 9 8 7 6 5 4 3 2 1

For those who are wild at heart
—A.G.

For D.M.
—J.M.

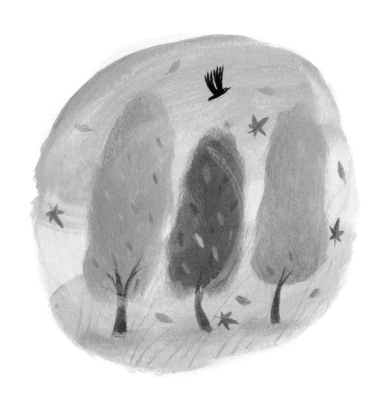

It started quietly, with a small flutter of leaves on the old oak tree.

They did not notice it as they napped on the porch. As they raced through the dust. As they played in the shade. No one noticed, but it was coming.

The leaves fluttered again, harder this time, and the ends of the branches shook.

The wren lifted her head. The crow flapped his wings. They felt something then . . . something swift and sweet. A breath of wind touched their feathers, and for an instant the air was not so heavy or so thick.

It was coming. Oh yes, it was coming.

The sky, just along the edge, changed from hazy blue to a soft shade of purple.

The cow swished her tail.

The pig flicked his ears.
Both turned to look as the purple spread across the blue like
a curtain.
It was coming. They knew it was coming.

In the air, the smell of dust suddenly mixed with a new
smell, one that was wild and clean.
The cat twitched her whiskers.
The dog sniffed with his nose.

They breathed deeply and let the wild smell flow through
them. Their eyes brightened and their tails flicked this way
and that, now wild too.

It was coming. They could tell it was coming.

In the purple sky, clouds gathered—only a few at first. Then more and more, until they were a thick, dark crowd.

The squirrel froze
on his tree.
    The mouse stood still
in the grass.

    They both watched as
the army of clouds marched
across the sky, swift and
sure. The clouds covered
the sun, and the day went
dark and cool.
    It was coming. Oh yes,
it was coming.

The breeze suddenly became a wind, blowing with gusts that flattened the grass and pulled at hair. The trees whipped this way and that, as if afraid.

On the porch, the grandmother stirred and opened her eyes. In the yard, the playing children looked up.

They all paused as they felt the strength of the wind, as it tugged at their sleeves and stung their eyes.

It was coming. It was coming and it was very close now.

A single drop of rain hit the dust and lay there in a tiny puddle. The wind died down, and for a moment, everything was still.

And all who were watching knew . . . it was here.

A single bolt of lightning streaked through the sky, cutting the air like a knife.

Crack!

Thunder boomed like a hundred drums, and the sound rolled across the ground like a wave.
Boom!

The wren and the crow darted for safety in the branches of the old oak tree.

The cow and the pig bolted for the shelter of the barn.

The cat and the dog raced together for the shed, where it was quiet and dark.

The squirrel and the mouse scampered toward holes, where it was darker still.

The children ran toward their grandmother on the porch, and huddled close.

Lightning cracked the sky with silver streaks. Thunder rolled and boomed, filling the flat land with its echoes. The wind wailed and howled, causing trees to bow down and the grass to ripple like the sea. The rain fell in a solid sheet, one that darkened the dust and turned it to mud. The air was wet and wild and full of sound.

It was here. It was here. It was here.

Then . . . as swiftly as it had come, it was gone. All that was left of its passing was a distant thrum of thunder, soft, like a whisper on the breeze.

The children, still huddled around their grandmother, slowly let go. They stood tall and blinked at the newness of their yard, at how quickly it had changed.

Almost as one, they smiled.

It ended quietly, with a last rumble in the air. They did not notice it as they danced in the mud. As they skipped through the puddles. As they smiled at the green of the grass.

The thunderstorm was gone.

Somewhere, though, deep in the hearts of the crow and the dog and the mouse, and deep in the minds of the playing children, the wonder of the storm remained.

For everyone knew . . . it would come again.